By Patricia MacLachlan and Emily MacLachlan Charest

Fiona Loves the Night

Illustrated by
Amanda Shepherd

JOANNA COTLER BOOKS
An Imprint of HarperCollins Publishers

Fiona kisses her mother good night.
She kisses her father.
She kisses Max, the dog.
Fiona sleeps.
She sleeps for a long time.

Then, when half a moon shines
through her window, Fiona wakes.
She gets up and turns off her night-light.
She turns off the lamp in the hall.
She looks out her window.

Now she
can see
the night.

Max watches her,
but he doesn't get up.

He knows where
she is going.

He knows
Fiona loves
the night.

Fiona opens her French doors.
The night wraps around her
like a velvet coat.

It is silent.
It is safe.

Stars slip across the sky.
They light up Fiona's night.

She looks for the Big Dipper.
She looks for the Little Dipper.

She looks for her bright North Star.

Fiona listens to the night sounds.

She hears the crickets' loud chirping.

Far off, she hears the soft sound

of a barred owl:

Who-whoo,

Who-whoo,

Who cooks
for you all?

And in the field a mockingbird begins an evening song:
first one song, then another, then back again.
He copies the songs of other birds.

Fiona calls to the mockingbird,
hoping he will copy her song.

He is quiet.

Then he begins his own song again.

Fiona walks across the grass to the garden.

The grass is **cool** and **wet**.

Fireflies **flash** in the dark.

Fiona runs through the fireflies, her arms out.
It is like running through stars.

A huge luna moth flutters

just above
her head.

Moonlight shines through
its lace green wings.
Fiona reaches up to touch it,

but it flutters away.

Fiona's night garden is blooming—the angel's trumpet and the moonflower that bloom only in the dark.

She touches the soft lamb's ear, silver in the light.
Behind it, a spider has built a web.
Droplets of water sit there like jewels.

Fiona counts the bats in the sky.

One,

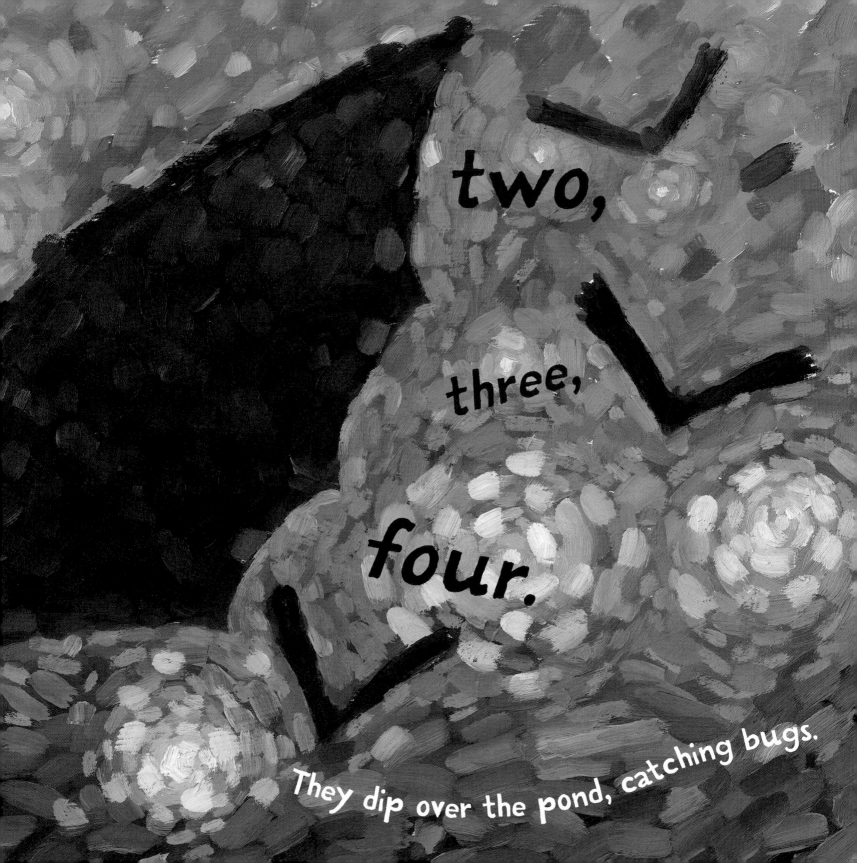

two,

three,

four.

They dip over the pond, catching bugs.

There is a moon in the
middle of the pond.

All around her the frogs
jump into the water,
making the moon wrinkle.

Plop.

Then, **suddenly**, Fiona stops at the edge of the meadow.
Ahead of her are eyes shining in the dark.

Is it the neighbor's cat?

A raccoon? **A coyote?**

The eyes come closer. **Closer.**

Fiona walks down the path to the meadow.
Tall grasses grow on either side.

She trails her hands along them.

swish,

swish,

swish,

swish.

"**Max!**"

cries Fiona happily.

She puts her arms
around him.
Max has come to
take her home.

The two of them walk up the path between the grasses, past the pond, through the garden, and into Fiona's bedroom.

Fiona gets into bed. Max curls up beside her.
Outside, the birds begin to sing.

It is almost
morning.

The bats are hanging upside down
in their bat houses.

The owl sleeps in its tree.

The luna moth folds its wings.

Fiona sleeps and dreams.
In her sleep she smiles
because she dreams about the night.

Fiona

loves

the

night.

This book is for Sofia,
from her mother and grandmother.
—P.M. and E.M.C.

For G, Poe, and Miss Kate
—A.S.

Fiona Loves the Night
Text copyright © 2007 by Patricia MacLachlan and Emily MacLachlan Charest
Illustrations copyright © 2007 by Amanda Shepherd
Manufactured in China. All rights reserved. No part of this book may be used or reproduced in any
manner whatsoever without written permission except in the case of brief quotations embodied in
critical articles and reviews. For information address HarperCollins Children's Books, a division of
HarperCollins Publishers, 1350 Avenue of the Americas, New York, NY 10019.
www.harpercollinschildrens.com

Library of Congress Cataloging-in-Publication Data
MacLachlan, Patricia.
   Fiona loves the night / by Patricia MacLachlan and Emily MacLachlan Charest ; illustrated by Amanda
Shepherd.— 1st ed.
      p.   cm.
   Summary: Fiona explores the nighttime wonders of the outdoors, from the sounds of the owl and
mockingbird to flowers that bloom only in the dark.
   ISBN-10: 0-06-057031-8 (trade bdg.) — ISBN-13: 978-0-06-057031-6 (trade bdg.)
   ISBN-10: 0-06-057032-6 (lib. bdg.) – ISBN-13: 978-0-06-057032-3 (lib. bdg.)
   [1. Night—Fiction. 2. Nature—Fiction.] I. Charest, Emily MacLachlan. II. Shepherd, Amanda, ill. III. Title.
PZ7.M2225 Fio 2007   2006021265
[E]—dc22

Typography by Neil Swaab
1 2 3 4 5 6 7 8 9 10
❖
First Edition